Cristina Salat
Peanut's Emergency

Is this an emergency?

Illustrated by Tammie Lyon

Whispering Coyote
A Charlesbridge Imprint

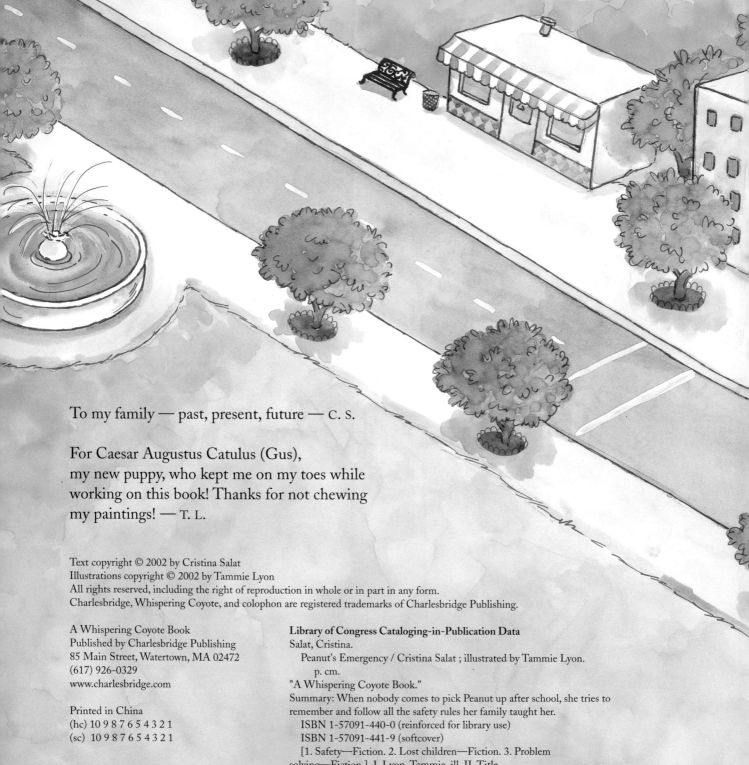

To my family — past, present, future — C. S.

For Caesar Augustus Catulus (Gus),
my new puppy, who kept me on my toes while
working on this book! Thanks for not chewing
my paintings! — T. L.

A Whispering Coyote Book
Published by Charlesbridge Publishing
85 Main Street, Watertown, MA 02472
(617) 926-0329
www.charlesbridge.com

Printed in China
(hc) 10 9 8 7 6 5 4 3 2 1
(sc) 10 9 8 7 6 5 4 3 2 1

Library of Congress Cataloging-in-Publication Data
Salat, Cristina.
    Peanut's Emergency / Cristina Salat ; illustrated by Tammie Lyon.
        p. cm.
"A Whispering Coyote Book."
Summary: When nobody comes to pick Peanut up after school, she tries to
remember and follow all the safety rules her family taught her.
    ISBN 1-57091-440-0 (reinforced for library use)
    ISBN 1-57091-441-9 (softcover)
    [1. Safety—Fiction. 2. Lost children—Fiction. 3. Problem
solving—Fiction.] I. Lyon, Tammie, ill. II. Title.
    PZ7.S14785 Pe 2002
    [E]—dc21   2001004377s

The illustrations in this book were painted in watercolor on Bristol Board.
The text type is set in Adobe Caslon and the display type is set in Dolores, designed by Tobias Frere-Jones.
Color separations were made by Ocean Graphic Company Ltd.
Printed and bound in China by Everbest Printing Company Ltd. through
Four Color Imports Ltd., Louisville, Kentucky
Production supervision by Brian G. Walker.
Designed by Susan M. Sherman.

"Be quiet, children, and listen," Ms. Sarah Anne says. I giggle with my best friend Honey. We wiggle in our seats. It is sunny outside, and I do not like being quiet. I want to be noisy and run.

School is out!

Honey and I twirl in circles
on the way out to the yard.

Shugga! Shugga!

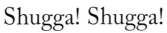

Dance! Dance!

We chase April butterflies until Honey's baby-sitter comes to pick her up.

Ryan leaves with his dad.

Rhonda leaves with her mom.

I wait.

Nobody comes for me.

I wait.
And wait.
I do not like waiting.
I swing high.

I climb near the tippy-toe top of the crooked tree.
I do not see anyone I know coming. Everybody from
my class is gone, and I am still waiting.
I watch Ms. Sarah Anne leave. I wave from up high,
but she does not see me.

I really do not like waiting.
It makes me grouchy.
I am getting very grouchy.
Red-hot, stamp-your-sneakers grouchy.

I head for the pay phone across the street. Mommy has put coins in the zipper pockets on my sneakers for emergency telephone calls.

There are many kinds of emergencies:

Fires!

Accidents!

Wild animals!

Shipwrecks!

I have never had an emergency. Is this one?

I unzip one sneaker pocket, then the other.
They are empty.

Someone must have stolen my money!
I only bought cupcakes at lunch once, maybe twice…
well, maybe three times….

"Do not use this money unless you have to,"
Mommy said when she put the coins into my
sneaker pockets. "That is a Safety Rule."
I think I have been bad.
Very, very bad.

This might be an emergency.
And my emergency money is gone.

Maybe I can call collect?
When you press "0" and say "I want to make a
collect call, please," the operator calls people for
you and makes them pay. You should only do
this in an emergency. My daddy says so.
Who should I call?

Tuesdays, Mommy is supposed to pick me up.
Unless she has a meeting.
Then Aunty Rosie picks me up.
Unless she has a dentist appointment.
Then Daddy picks me up.
Unless he is out of town. . . .
Where is everybody?!

I am mad! I am very, very mad!
I yell at the operator, "This is Peanut! Get me my mommy!"
She says, "What is the phone number, dear?"

what is the phone number, dear?

I know my number. I know lots of numbers.
Home numbers and office numbers, even the numbers
for Honey and Ryan, my best friends.
Grandpa always says I have a head for numbers.
"What is the number, dear?"
I cannot remember a single one.

What should I do?
"Please help me find my puppy," says a man.
He is a big, friendly person, and I love puppies.
L-O-V-E, love!
But I am supposed to be careful with strangers.
That is a Safety Rule. Strangers can pretend to be nice when they really are not.
The puppy person smiles and reaches for my hand.

"I DO NOT TALK TO STRANGERS!"
People across the street turn to look.
The stranger's smile fades.
If a stranger bothers me, I am supposed
to get someplace safe and tell!

I run around the corner into a store.
Mommy buys "coffee to go" here.
Mrs. Yee is not a stranger. I think.
"Nobody came to get me!" I cry.
"And I don't have any money,
I can't remember my phone number,
and a stranger is talking to me!"
I am so upset, I start to hiccup.

"Oh my," Mrs. Yee says.
"Is this an emergency?" I whisper.
Mrs. Yee hands me a cherry sucker
and unwraps a grape one for herself.
"Maybe, maybe not," she says.
"In either case, we should not panic."

She hoists a big book onto the counter.
"What is your name?"
"Peanut Nwanda. P-e-a-n-u-t N-w-a-n-d-a."
At least I have not forgotten how to spell.
There is only one Nwanda family
on our street in the big book.
Mrs. Yee dials.
No one is home.

"Who else can we call?"
"Grandpa," I say. But it does not say Grandpa in
the big book and I can't remember Grandpa's
other name. "Grandpa is Mommy's father,"
I tell Mrs. Yee. But that does not help her.

I am sad.
I am very, very sad.
Icy silver sad.

It is almost night.
"I cannot leave you here," she says.
"I will take you home with me."
"I am not supposed to go to anyone's house without
telling my mother," I say. "That is a Safety Rule."
Mrs. Yee scratches her head. "I suppose we could
call the police," she says.

Police can help with an emergency.
Their phone number is 911.
The police station is on Maple Street.
How will Mommy or Daddy or Aunty Rosie
or Grandpa find me there?
Also, there are lots of strangers at a police station.
Big, scary strangers.
I am worried.
Queasy-orange-sick-to-my-stomach worried.

Mrs. Yee calls my house one more time.

Mommy answers! I can hear her voice from across the counter!
"My car broke down!" she says. "I will be right there!"

A few minutes later Mommy rushes in.
She scoops me up. I am so happy to see her,
I forget I was ever mad.
"Why did you wander off?" she cries, squeezing me tight.
"I called the whole neighborhood!
Daddy and Aunty Rosie were searching everywhere!"

I feel bad. Very, very bad.
Slimy green, curl-your-toes bad.
It was an emergency, and I did it wrong.

Everybody is at our house.
"There is our lost Peanut!" Grandpa cries.
"I was not lost," I say softly. "I was in Mrs. Yee's store."
Daddy swoops me into an eagle glide, singing,
"Our brave Peanut has found her way home!"
"Thank goodness," Aunty Rosie laughs.
"My turn for a hug!"

My family makes a welcome-home feast.
Everybody wants to hear where I was
and what I did when I was "lost."
I tell them. I do not leave anything out.
Grandpa grins. "Peanut is smart! S-m-a-r-t!
Takes after me!"
Aunty Rosie writes down everybody's name, address,
and phone number.

Mommy gets more coins. They put the list and coins
into my left sneaker pocket.
"For emergencies only," Mommy says,
and gives me the eye.
Then she puts more quarters into the zipper pocket
on my right sneaker.
"For cupcakes," she smiles.

I frown. Why are they being so nice?
It is important to know what to do in an emergency,
and to do it! That is a Safety Rule!
Everybody is acting wrong!

I get mad.
Very, very mad.
Red-hot mad!

"I am not brave or smart," I tell them,
stamping my sneakers. "I was bad!
I spent my emergency money. I wandered off.
I could not remember anybody's phone number—
not a single one! I think you should punish me!"

"Did you go anywhere with a stranger?" Aunty Rosie asks.
I shake my head.
At least I did not do that.

"Did you get help when you needed it?" Daddy asks.
I nod.
Mrs. Yee helped me.

"Did you make it home safe and sound?" Grandpa asks.
I nod again.
"Well, then," he chuckles. "You did a good deal right!"

Mommy turns my face to look at her.
"You are very, very good," she says, not
sounding disappointed at all.
"In an emergency, somebody brave and smart
keeps thinking and trying until they find a way
to get safe. That is what you did."
"Well…," I say.
I guess that is true.

"And now the emergency is o-v-e-r, over!"
Grandpa spells. "I think I need another hug."
Grandpa and Aunty Rosie and Mommy
and Daddy and I are happy the
emergency is over.
We are very, very happy!
Everyone is so sunshine happy,
stamp-your-sneakers feeling good,
we circle the kitchen.
Shugga! Shugga!
Dance! Dance!